SOMEONE'S NEAR

Mamie Farrar Vick

AuthorHouse™
1663 Liberty Drive
Bloomington, IN 47403
www.authorhouse.com
Phone: 1-800-839-8640

Published by AuthorHouse 09/30/2011

ISBN: 978-1-4670-4124-9 (sc)

Any people depicted in stock imagery provided by Thinkstock are models,
and such images are being used for illustrative purposes only.
Certain stock imagery © Thinkstock.

This book is printed on acid-free paper.

Because of the dynamic nature of the Internet, any web addresses or links contained in this book may have changed
since publication and may no longer be valid. The views expressed in this work are solely those of the author and do not
necessarily reflect the views of the publisher, and the publisher hereby disclaims any responsibility for them.

authorHOUSE®

Someone's Near

I can hear you breathing.

Somebody's near!

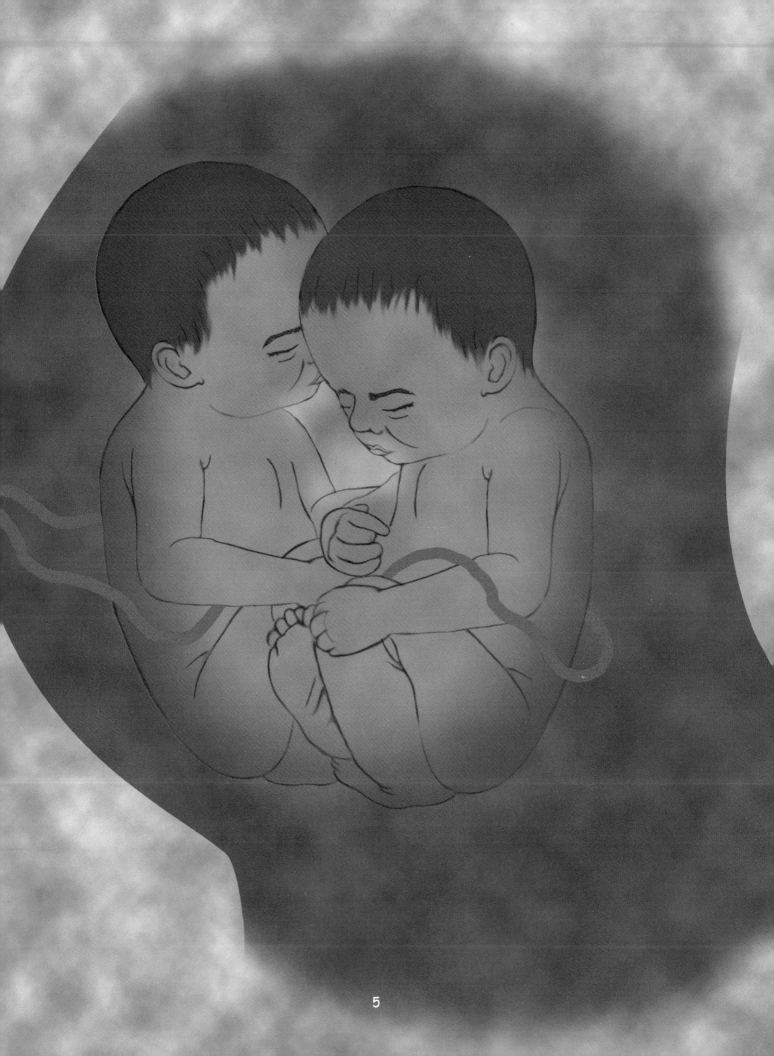

I can hear your heart beating.

Somebody's near!

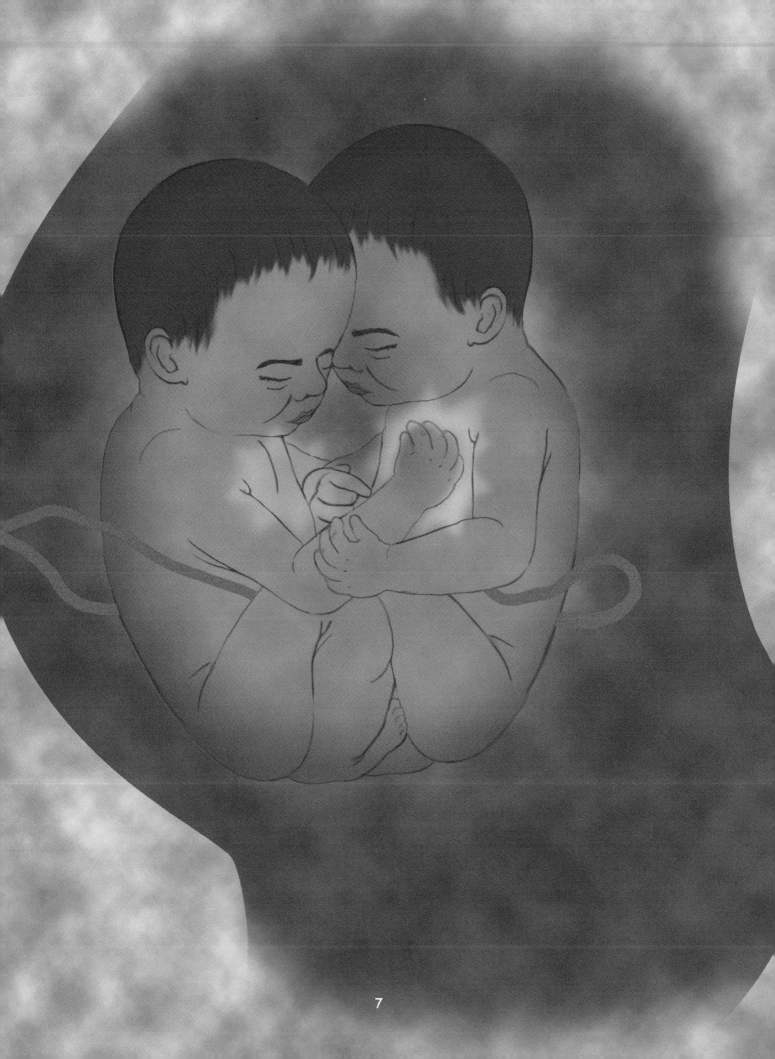

I can feel you moving.

Somebody's near!

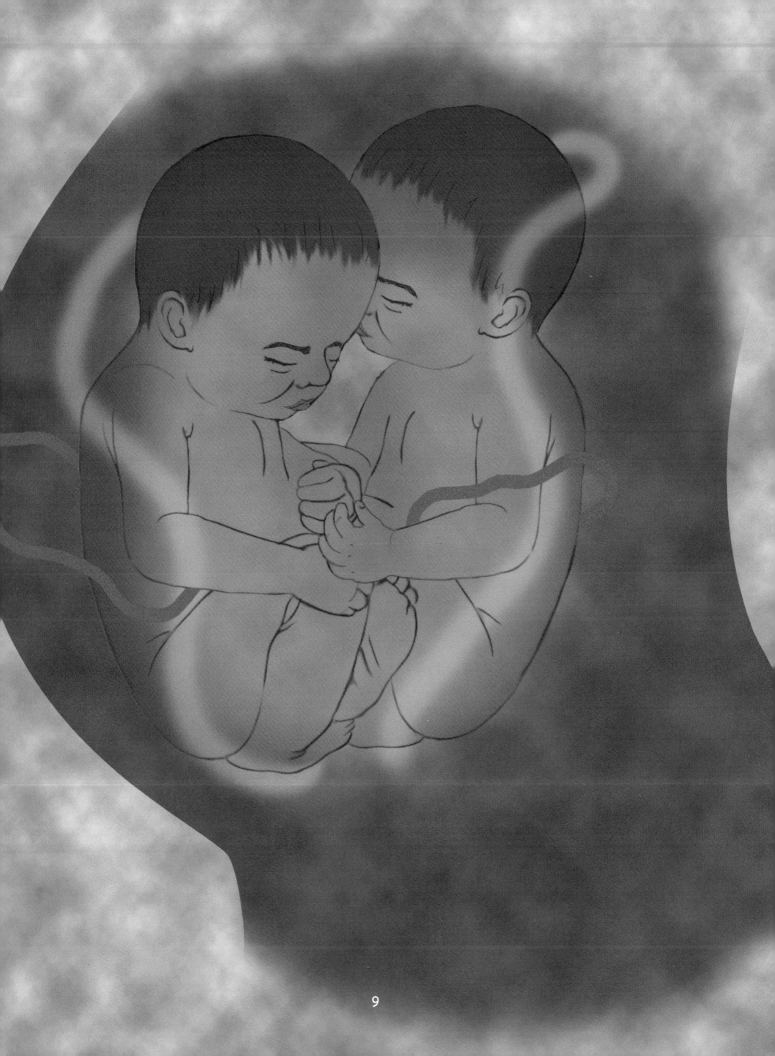

Boy, I am getting hungry!

Somebody's near!

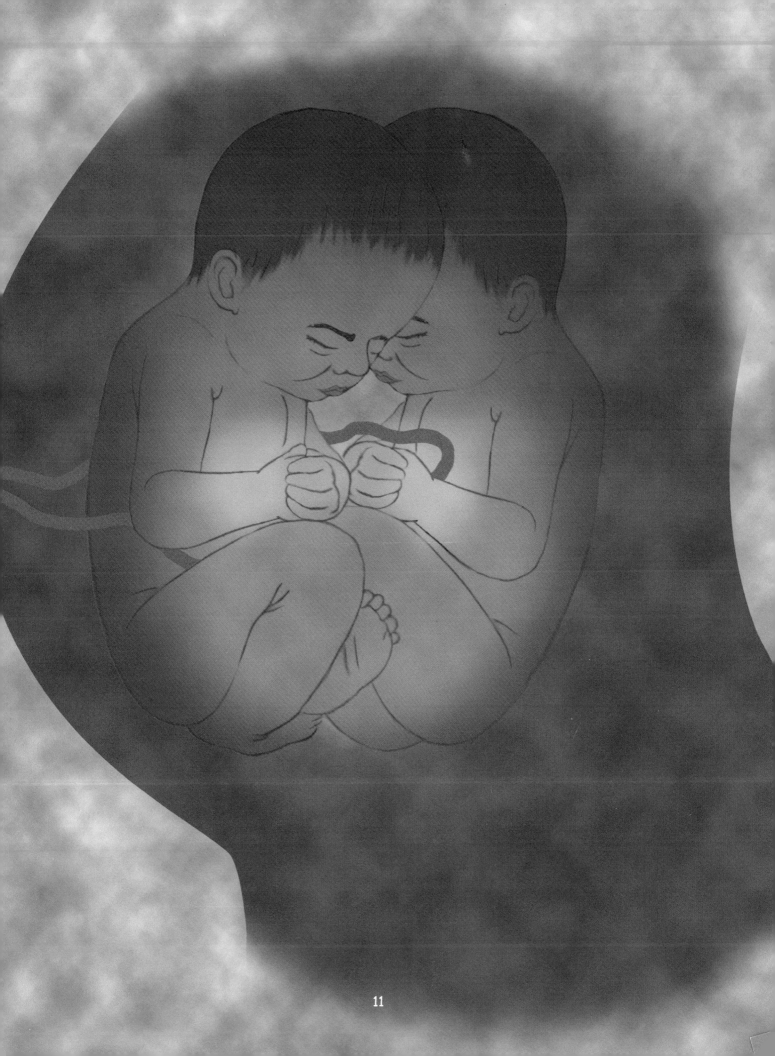

Hey, it's getting crowded in here.

Somebody's near!

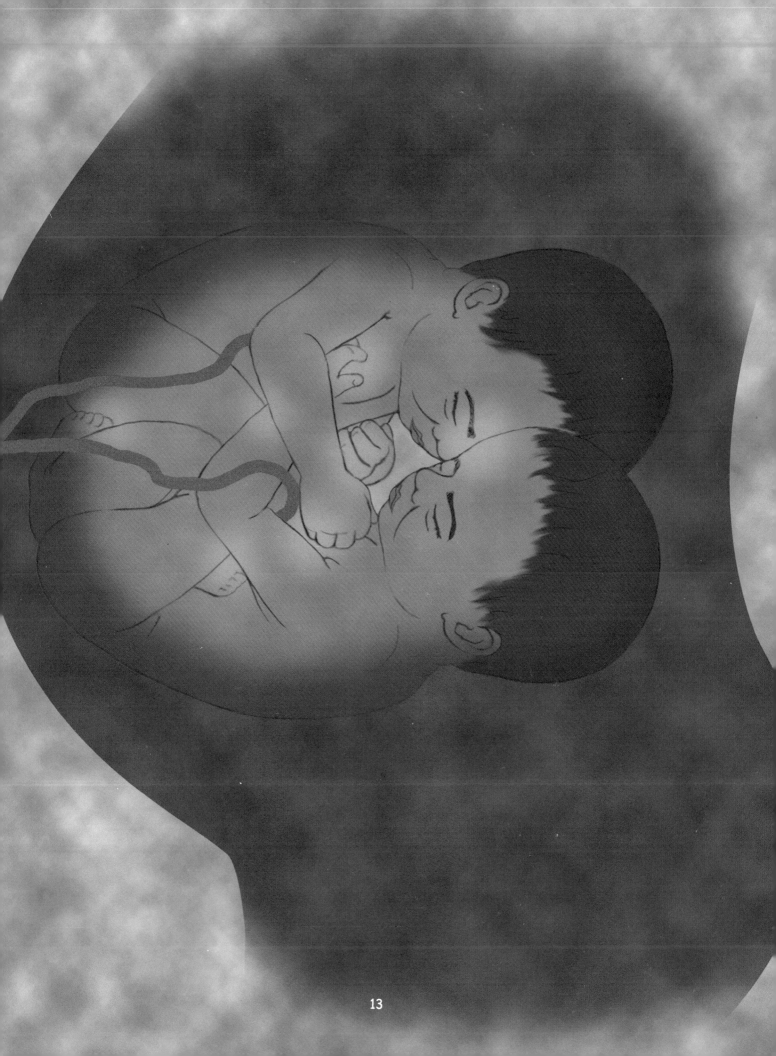

I can't move my arms and legs.

Somebody's near!

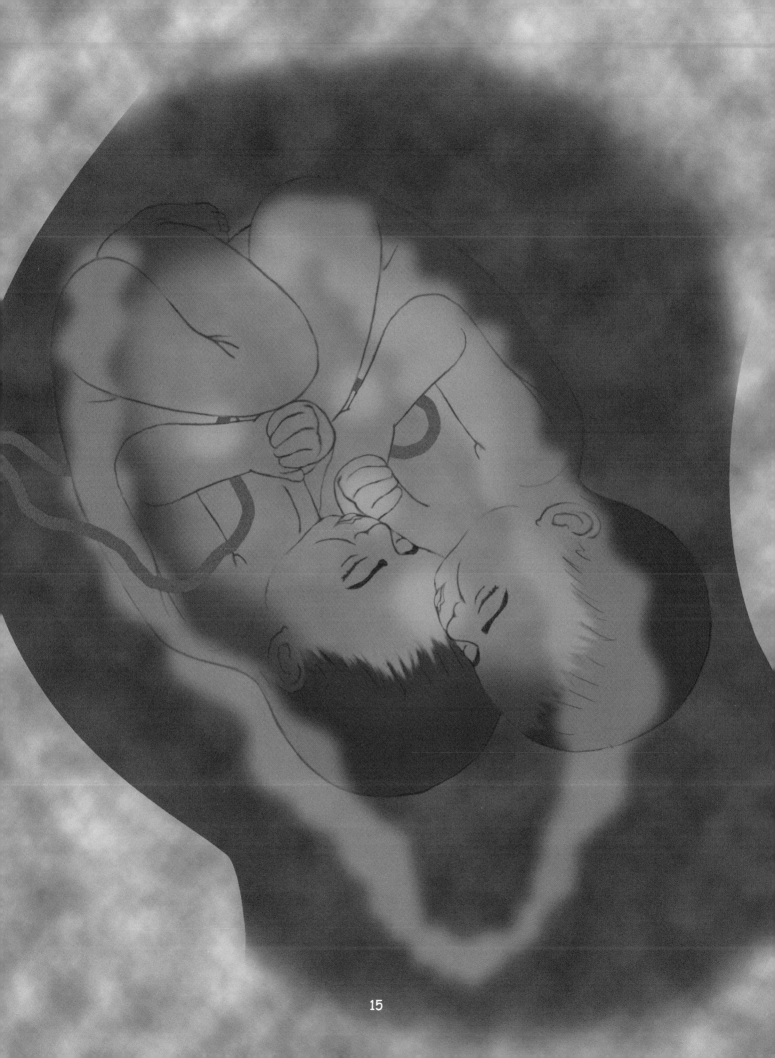

Ouch! What's that?

Somebody's near!

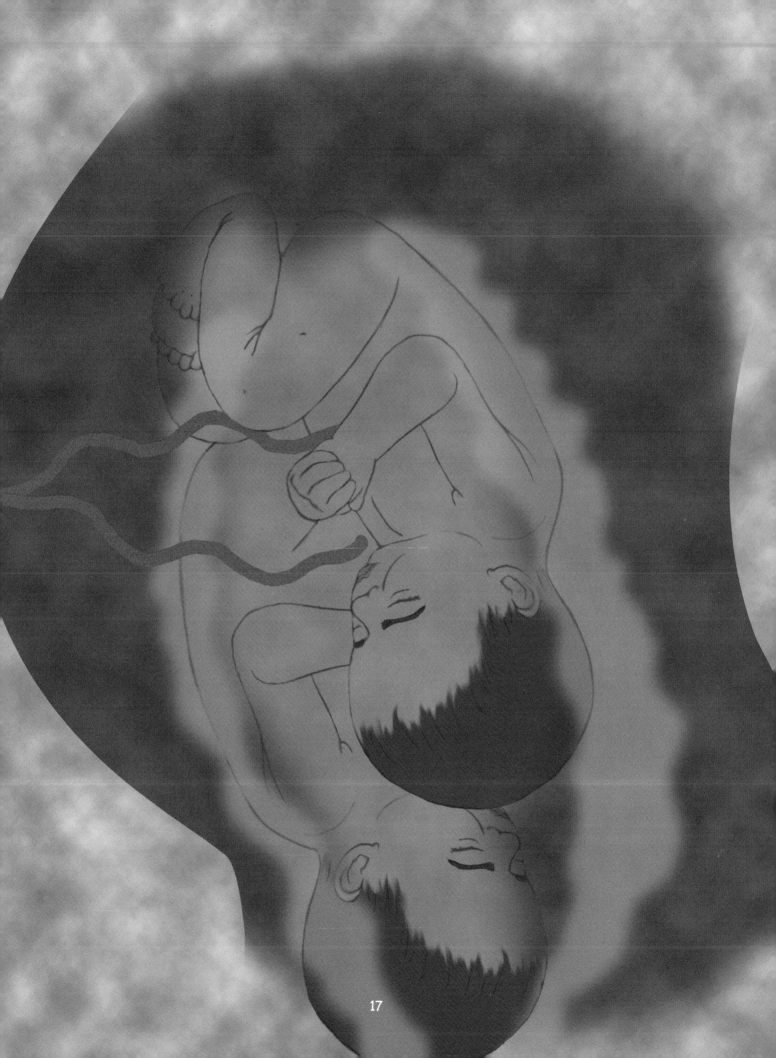

Hey, where did you go?

Nobody's near.

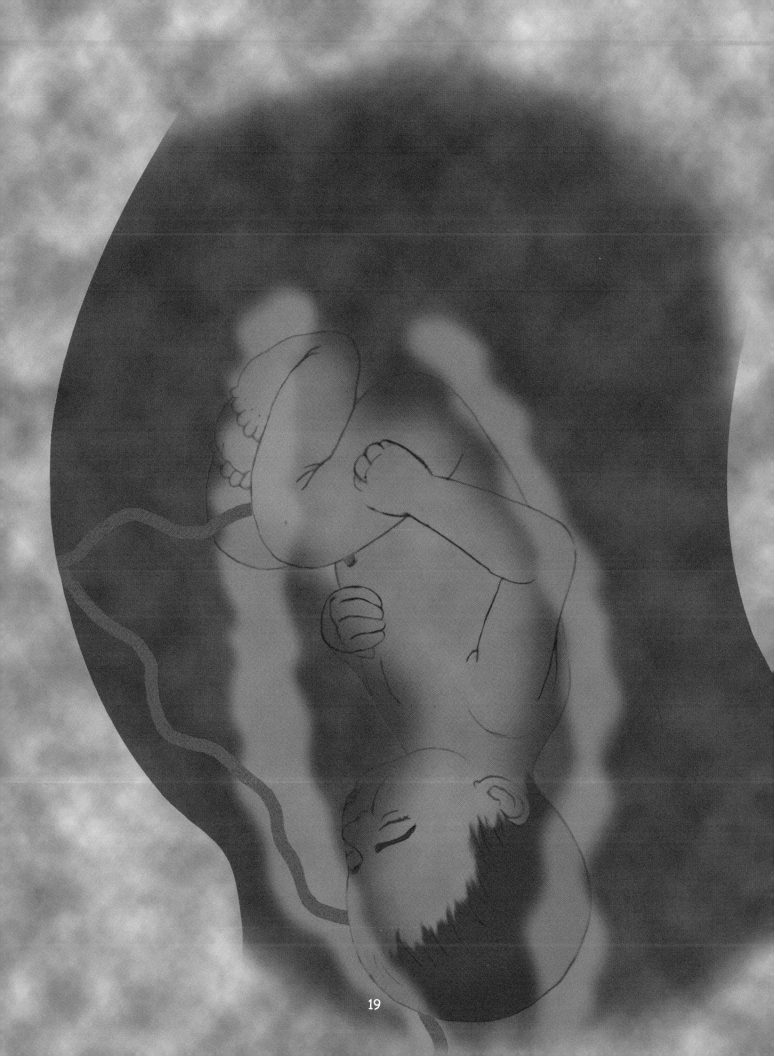

Wait for me; I'm coming too.

Somebody's near!

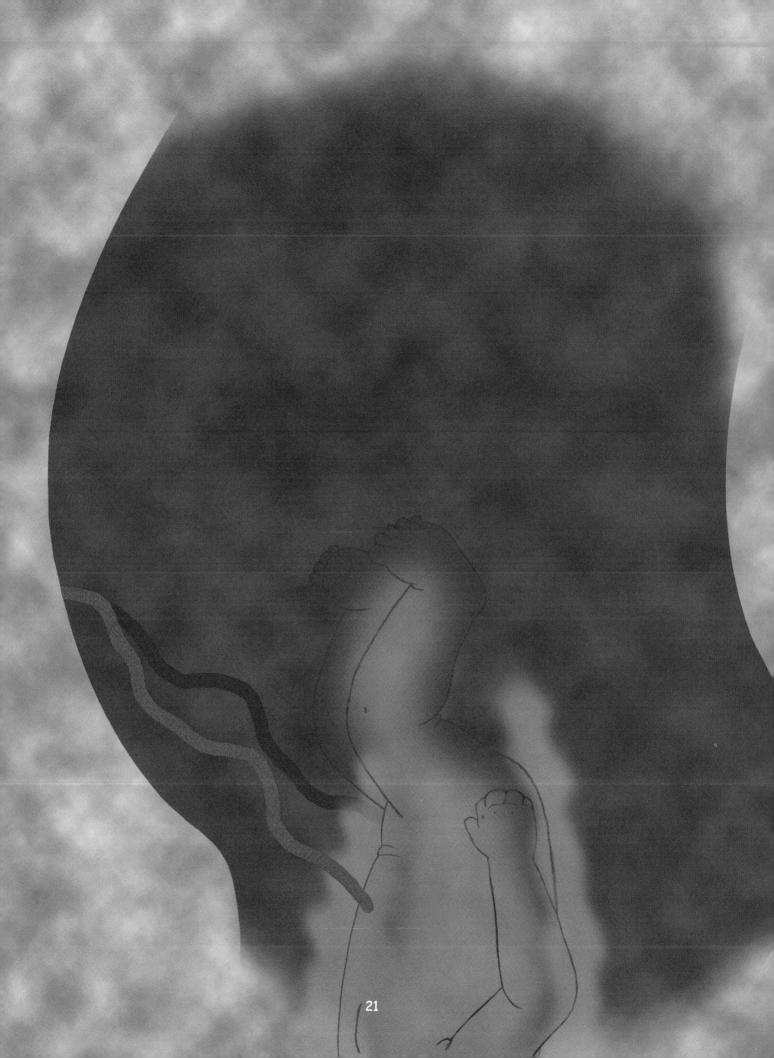

Hello, I'm Yasmine!

Hi, I'm Myiane!

CPSIA information can be obtained
at www.ICGtesting.com
Printed in the USA
LVIC032232250912

300257LV00006B